Mustachio

the **magician** who couldn't pull a **rabbit** out of her **hat**

C a r t e s w i c k

blah!

blah!

blah!

for

LILLI

&

DIEGO

&

MOM

&

DAD

&

FAR

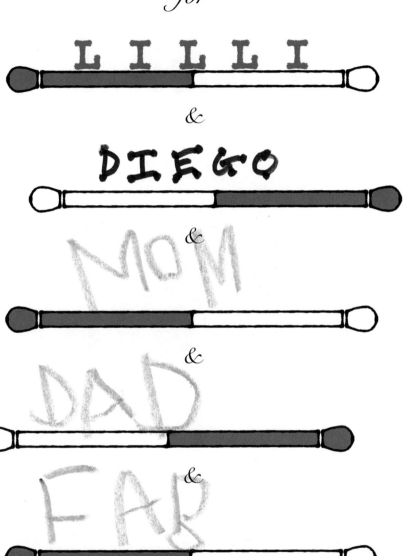

Mustachio was a **magician**.

Her best trick was
to make herself...

...disappear!

ta-da!

She was so good at it
that no one even knew
when she was doing it.

So she wore a
mustache,

to let people know
she was there.

That's why they called her

Mustachio!

The one trick that Mustachio couldn't do

was pull a rabbit out of her hat.

She tried,
and she tried,

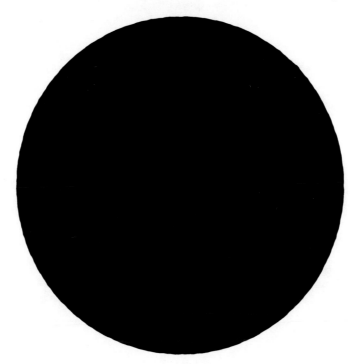

but every time
she reached inside...

...something else came out.

???

???

???

??? ??? co-kee!

She went to other magicians for advice.

"I always give *my* hat a good *shake* first,"

one magician told her.

Mustachio gave her hat a good *shake*

shake!

shake!

shake!

shake!

then reached inside...

...and pulled out a
tennis racket!

Another magician
asked her,

"Did you try
tapping the
hat with your
wand?"

Mustachio *tapped* her hat with her wand

then reached inside...

...and pulled out a **toothbrush!**

??? ??? ??? ??? ???

She didn't know what to do.

Mustachio was set to perform at

Lilli's 4th Birthday Party!

It would be her **first** performance.

She *hoped* that it wouldn't be her last.

"If I **dazzle** the audience with my *other* tricks," she thought,

"then maybe they won't even *ask* me to pull a rabbit out of my hat!"

So she made herself...

oooh!

oooh!

oooh!

...disappear!

oooh!

Then she made her
mustache . . .

ahhh!

ahhh!

...change colors!

ahhh!

ahhh!

She made all of the balloons pop!

pop!

pop!

pop!

pop!

pop!

pop!

pop!

pop!

Then she made them all reappear!

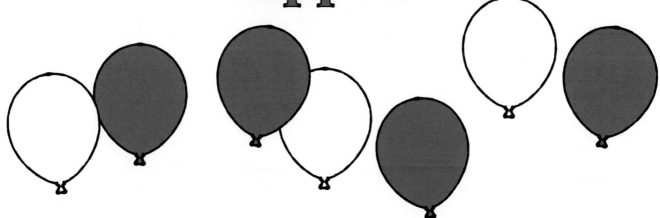

It was time for her *grand finale.* But then,

"Pull a rabbit out of your hat!"

someone shouted.

Others joined in.

"Yeah! Pull a rabbit out of your hat!"

Mustachio didn't know *what* to do.

She tried to remember what the other magicians had told her. She **shook** her wand then *tapped* her *mustache.*

shake!

shake!

shake!

tap!

tap!

tap!

Then she reached inside her hat...

...and she felt **long ears!** But they weren't rabbit ears. *Instead,*

gasp!

gasp!

they were **kangaroo** ears! And the kangaroo did *not* like having her ears pulled.

uh-oh...

She *kicked* over the presents and *smushed* the cake with her tail

whoosh!

squish!

arf!

then tucked the family dog into her pouch and *hopped* off down the street!

arf?

Mustachio wanted to disappear forever. But then she heard,

woo!

woo!

"WOOOO!!!!"

woo!

woo!

woo!

woo!

woo!

The audience was cheering!

"We've seen magicians pull rabbits out of their hats before, but we've *never* seen a magician pull out a **kangaroo!**"

"What **else** can you pull out?!" someone asked.

"Can you perform at *my* birthday party?!"

Mustachio helped catch the kangaroo and retrieve the family dog.

arf!

And she had to promise not to cause *quite* so much mayhem at her next performance.

But soon she had birthday parties lined up for weeks.

Everyone wanted to see what would happen next with

Mustachio,

the magician who couldn't pull a rabbit out of her hat.

Made in the USA
Middletown, DE
02 April 2022

63506159R00020